Once upon a time, a boy called Bruno wished for his very own guinea pig.

Not so far away, in a little glass box, a tiny guinea pig

waited for his Big Person to come and find him...

For my dad

First published 2014 by Walker Books Ltd
87 Vauxhall Walk, London SE11 5HJ

2 4 6 8 10 9 7 5 3 1

© 2014 Sheena Dempsey

The right of Sheena Dempsey to be identified as author/illustrator
respectively of this work has been asserted by her in accordance
with the Copyright, Designs and Patents Act 1988

This book has been typeset in Caecilia

Printed in China

British Library Cataloguing in Publication Data:

a catalogue record for this book is available
from the British Library

ISBN 978-1-4063-3616-0

www.walker.co.uk

TO DO:
1. Get my guinea pig
2. Play lots of games

some are spotty

BRUNO and TITCH

The Tale of a Boy and His Guinea Pig

SHEENA DEMPSEY

WALKER BOOKS
AND SUBSIDIARIES
LONDON · BOSTON · SYDNEY · AUCKLAND

I've been waiting three human weeks for
a Big Person to come and bring me home.
In guinea pig time, that's almost a year.
Which is a VERY long time to wait.

No matter how hard I try
(and I try R-E-A-L-L-Y hard) …

the Big People always choose some other guinea pig instead.

Here's another Big Person right now.

I bet he's not here for me though. They never are.

Wait! Maybe ... maybe he IS here for me!

It's finally happening!
My very own Big Person AT LAST!

LOOK!

A house ... a real, live Big Person house.

I can't believe it. I've made it.

"Welcome to your new home, Titch!" said Bruno.

My new home is ... different.

Bruno eats strange food. He gets up very early.

And we don't always like the same things.

More than anything,
Bruno likes to play, A LOT.
And I love to play as much
as the next guinea pig ...
but there's only
so much
of the

Bouncing-
Very-High
game

I can take ...

This is not fun for me.

or the
Very-Scary-
Balloon
game ...

I like to stay on the ground
where my favourite
game is hiding.
It's quiet.
Not too HIGH ...
or bouncy ...
or *fast*.

Beware!
Dangerous
Aminals!

When we're not playing, Bruno and me
look at stuff together.

And we make all
kinds of important things.

Guinea Pig Air

← Like this.
It's an airy plane.

PHYSICS
of
FLIGHT

So even though we're different,
I think me and Bruno are
becoming the best of friends.

At least that's what I thought...

This morning, Bruno started
acting all strange.

He looked at me with
his BIG eye.

He drew some pictures
I didn't understand.

What's he *doing*
in there?

Maybe Bruno is bored of me already...
Is he going to get rid of me?

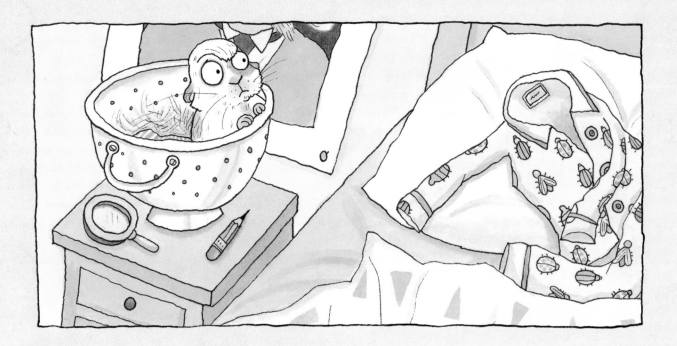

Where did he go?

Why hasn't he taken me
out of my bed yet?
This is not a good sign.

Maybe
he doesn't want
to be friends anymore?

Here he comes...

Please don't send me back to the glass box!

LOOK! A Guinea Pig Palace!

In all my guinea pig life (3 months and 3 weeks),
I've never seen anything so incredible!
"Behold my great guinea pig
palace of fun, Titch!
I hope you like it,"
said Bruno.

Only a true best friend could know
all of my favourite things.

My own jacuzzi.

A fruit salad bar.

(So delicious.)

Some privacy.

(I really need that.)

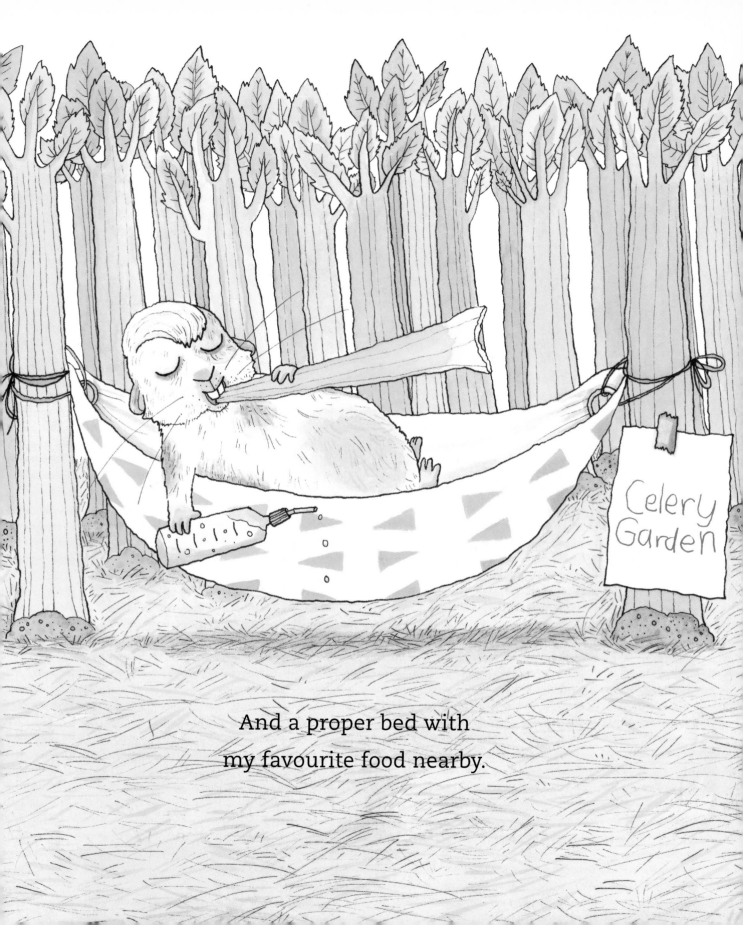

And a proper bed with
my favourite food nearby.

I waited a long time for my Big Person.

But now I have Bruno. And he has me.